DANGER GUYS

GUYS

On Ice

DANGER GUYS
On Ice

by Tony Abbott
illustrated by Joanne Scribner

HarperTrophy
A Division of HarperCollinsPublishers

Library of Congress Cataloging-in-Publication Data
Abbott, Tony.
    Danger Guys on ice/ by Tony Abbott ; illustrated by Joanne Scribner.
        p.   cm.
    Summary: During a ski trip, Noodle and Zeek find themselves trapped in
an icy mountain cave with an evil scientist and his army of frozen cavemen.
    ISBN 0-06-442010-8 (pbk.)
    [1. Adventure and adventures—Fiction.   2. Skis and skiing—Fiction .]
I. Scribner, Joanne, ill.   II. Title.   III. Series.
PZ7.A1587Das   1995   95-671
Fic—dc20   CIP
                                                                                AC

First Harper Trophy edition, 1995.

With love

for my mother and father

for starting off my life of books

—T. A.

Thanks to Nick Krenitsky and HarperCollins

—J. S.

ONE

It all happened in a flash.

It was my best friend Zeek's birthday. I was standing on his doorstep, trying to ring the doorbell.

Under one arm was some of my skiing gear. Skis, poles, and boots. Under the other arm was the rest of my skiing gear. Gloves, goggles, and ski hat.

In my teeth was a half-eaten Gold Bar Waffle Deluxe ice cream bar. The kind wrapped in gold foil.

I love waffles in any form. From plain waffles to waffle sandwiches to waffle cookies to waffle chips, waffles are my absolute favorite food.

Anyway, I was just working loose some fingers to press the doorbell.

Then it happened.

KA-FLOOOM!

The door blasted open, and I was suddenly on my back. Some bug-faced thing all dressed in ski gear flew right across my legs, out the door, and onto the front lawn. Snow sprayed up behind it.

"Mom!" called Zeek's sister, Emily, from the living room. "Zeek's being dangerous again!"

Ah, so it was Zeek! Yeah, he's dangerous. Well, I am, too. We have this danger thing. It just takes over, and we start doing incredible action stuff. It's the way we are.

"He almost killed Noodle!" she added.

Well, yeah, that's true, too. I looked down at the black ski marks across my jeans and the ice cream smear on my jacket.

But when you love danger as much as Zeek and I do, nearly getting killed is all part of it—part of being an official Danger Guy.

2

"Zeek-eek-eek! Pilinsky-insky!" he yelled across the lawn. "Gold-old medal-edal-edal!"

That's Zeekie. Amazing sports guy.

I scraped myself off the doorstep, picked up my stuff, and limped over to him.

He pulled up his bug-face ski mask. "Yaaaah!" he shouted, like a crowd cheering.

I finished what was left of my ice cream bar and folded the foil wrapper into a circle. I gave it to him. "Gold medal," I said. "Happy birthday."

"Thanks, Nood." He smiled big and popped it into the pocket of his Danger Guy jacket.

"Check out what my mom and dad got me," he said. "Aren't these skis cool? And this mask?" He pulled the green mask over his face, flexed his arms, and posed like somebody from a comic book. "I look like a superhero, don't I?"

"Yeah," I said, "Bug Boy." I laughed.

Zeek pushed the mask up to his forehead again, looked straight at me, and made a face.

That's another thing about Zeek. His faces crack me up. He can do this tiny smile that no one else can see. He does it in class a lot when our teacher, Mr. Strunk, isn't looking. It's like a secret code.

He was doing one of those smiles now.

Then he pointed up over the trees at the big purple-and-white mountain in the distance. "Look, Noodle. Snow. Lots of it. That's where my birthday ski party is going to be. My parents tried to keep it a surprise, but I figured it out."

"Of course you did," I said. "You can't surprise Danger Guys. We're ready for anything."

"Yeah," he said. "We save the surprises for bad guys!"

Zeek nodded at the skis under my arm. "Are you planning to build something, Noodle?"

I looked down at the chipped, brown

4

boards I was holding. "These were my dad's skis when he was a kid," I explained.

"Your dad is that old? They look like scrap lumber! And those boots have *laces*! Wow, are those, like, the first ski boots ever made?"

"Skiing is a very ancient sport," I said. "Remember what Mr. Vazny used to say?"

Zeek froze. "*Mr. Vazny!* You mean our old science teacher? Before he sneezed his brain loose and tried to blow up our school?"

I nodded. "He said that people have been skiing since prehistoric times."

I shivered, remembering how we found our teacher's secret laboratory under Mayville School and how he made us call him Dr. Morbius. When he tried to blow up the school, Zeek and I had to fly all over the galaxy in a rocket to stop him.

"The Sneezemeister!" Zeek whispered. "I'll *never* forget his face."

Yeah. Wispy hair. Evil grin. Drippy nose.

Mr. Vazny's sneezes were like nuclear explosions!

"He sure did have a sinus problem," I said. "Now whenever anybody sneezes, I break into a sweat."

"Me too," said Zeek. "I even scare myself when I get a runny nose!"

I shivered again. "Good thing the army locked him up."

"I hope they threw away the key."

Beep-beep! Zeek's dad pulled their mini-van out of the garage. We ran over and helped to pack up.

Two hours later, we tumbled out of the van in front of a giant log cabin. Zeek's mom, dad, and sister, Emily, went inside to set up for the party.

I stayed outside with Zeek. There was a plaque on the front of the building. " 'Mine Mountain Lodge,' " I read. "Cool! It says this mountain used to be the site of an old mineral mine. And this lodge was the owner's house."

I looked up. Smoke was rising from the chimney. It looked warm inside. It made me hungry.

"Let's go in," I said. "Maybe they have food."

"No way!" said Zeek, pulling me over to the bottom of the slope. A blast of cold air rushed down the mountain and hit me in the face. I could see my breath. It was going to be one freezing-cold day.

Zeek snapped on his skis. "Noodle, the good news is that if we jump on the ski lift now, we'll have time for one quick run before the party!"

Mine Mountain rose straight up like a giant snowy head. The ski-lift cable dangled like a skinny wire all the way to the top.

"And what's the bad news?" I mumbled.

Just then a man came running down from the ski lift. He was a little funny-looking. Well, a lot funny-looking. He wore thick pink glasses and had a fluffy black mustache and strange hair. It was bright red and growing straight up.

Bad hair day, I thought.

Besides that, he was squeezing his nose tight as if he had a cold. Oh, yeah, I forgot to mention that his nose was big and pink and round.

Zeek nudged me. "Probably a surprise clown my parents hired for my party," he whispered. "Don't let on I figured it out."

"Um, excuse me," I said. "How's the skiing today?"

"Dangerous!" the clown muttered under his mustache. He turned away quickly and disappeared behind the lodge.

I turned to Zeek. "If he's a clown, how come I'm not laughing?" I started back to the lodge. "I'm going to eat some cake."

I didn't move fast enough. Before I knew it, I was sitting next to Zeek in a little chair sailing high above the snow.

Zeek took a deep breath and gazed around. "Ah, what a great day!"

My stomach didn't think so. We were

climbing higher and higher in that dinky little lift chair. I tried not to think about how high we were. Or how far away from the lodge we were going. After all, this was Zeek's day, and he was—

GRRR! A motor growled and sputtered down below. We watched as the clown zoomed up the mountain on a sleek blue snowmobile.

"Hey, where's he going?" said Zeek. "Shouldn't he be tying balloons or something?"

POP! A chunk of something fell off our ski lift. I think it was a chunk of ski lift.

"Zeek? This doesn't look good—"

ERRRCH! The lift jerked to a stop.

It swung there for a second or two.

I looked at Zeek. He looked at me.

"Oh." My voice went sort of weak. "Now I know what the bad news is. . . ."

KA-CHANK!—The lift cable suddenly swung loose, and we dropped like stones to the icy ground below.

TWO

My whole life flashed before my eyes.

WHOOSH!

It didn't take very long.

By the time I started to scream—*Floo!*—I couldn't. My mouth was full of snow, and I was buried headfirst in a deep drift, a mess of skis and poles and arms and legs.

"I'm smushed!" I cried, yanking my head out.

But, as Zeek would say, that was the *good* news.

The bad news was—no Zeek.

His skis were resting on the snow close by, but he wasn't in them.

I pulled myself together, stood up in my

skis on a little mound of snow, and looked all around. There wasn't anyone in sight. "Zeekie!" I yelled.

"Maa-rrrrmmmf!" came the answer.

I looked down. There was a little pink mouth sticking out between my skis.

"Maa-rrrrmmmf!" it said again.

"Zeek!" I stepped off the mound and started digging around the mouth. A minute later Zeek burst out of the snow.

"Wha-wha-what happened?" he cried.

"We fell," I said. "About fifty feet. From there." I pointed up at the lift. "I knew it would break, I just knew it!"

"Hey!" Zeek shouted. "My skis!"

I whirled around. His skis were starting to slide across the snow down toward the lodge.

"I'll get them," I cried. I dug my poles deep into the snow. I leaped forward. My style was terrific.

Umph! My skis didn't move. I fell on my face.

"Ski, Noodle! Ski!" Zeek yelled.

I tugged and tugged at my legs. They didn't budge. It was like I was glued to the snow.

Meanwhile Zeek's skis were zooming downhill as though an invisible skier was wearing them. They were really flying.

I tried to lift my legs again. "Aren't skis supposed to *slide*?" Finally, one ski pulled loose. Big clumps of snow were stuck to the bottom.

"You need to wax them up," said Zeek in a kind of flat voice. "See mine?" He pointed to his skis, just vanishing over a distant ridge. "Mine are waxed great."

"Oh," I said. "I guess my dad did say something about *wax*, but I thought he said *snacks*, so I grabbed an ice cream bar." I laughed a little.

Zeek didn't think it was too funny.

Then I had an idea. "Hey, since my skis don't slide too well, maybe we can make a signal."

13

I took off my skis and formed an X in the snow with them. "This way, anybody looking for us will see them. My dad will be so proud I used his skis."

"Yeah," said Zeek, still staring at the spot where his own skis had disappeared. "That's the main thing. Come on, let's go."

I took a step. *SLUP!* My right foot, with just a sock on it, plunged deep into the snow.

"My boot got untied in the fall," I said, shivering. Zeek rolled his eyes while I pulled the boot from the snow, stuck my wet foot back in, and retied the laces.

We slowly started down the mountain, but we stopped at the top of a high ridge.

I looked over it. "The good news is, we can see the lodge."

Zeek nodded. "The bad news is, we can't get there from here."

He was right. Just below the ridge a deep chasm ran like a gash across the mountain. It was total ice all the way down, and so deep we couldn't see the bottom.

"I guess the snow buried the sign," Zeek said.

"What sign?"

"The one that says 'Pit of Death—This Way.' "

"Very funny," I said. "Let's hit the trail."

Zeek looked around and frowned. "What trail?"

I smiled. "The one *you're* going to make and *I'm* going to follow."

"Oh," he said. "That trail."

We started back up around the ravine. It took us a long time, plowing through the deep snow. An icy wind bit into our faces.

"It's getting colder," Zeek said.

"At least it's not snowing."

That instant, a tiny snowflake fluttered down and landed on the tip of my nose.

"Never mind," I said.

Two minutes later we were in the fiercest blizzard this side of the Ice Age.

The air was white with huge flakes. The temperature zoomed down. Snow was freezing on my eyelashes. I didn't like it.

Rrrrrr! Something rumbled.

I didn't like that, either.

Zeek turned. "Not that old stomach joke, Noodle? You see the lodge and you think log cabin and then you think maple syrup, and then you think waffles. And of course when *you* think waffles, your *stomach* thinks waffles and—"

RRRRRRRRR! The ground quaked, and the air roared all around us.

"Um . . . that's not me, Zeek," I said. "Really."

The sound was coming from behind us. It was deep and booming, like a thousand bulldozers starting up. Or a stampede of cattle.

But I knew it wasn't bulldozers or cattle. They don't have those in the mountains.

They have something else in the mountains.

"SNOW!" I screamed.

"SNOW COMING FAST!" Zeek screamed.

"AVALANCHE!" we both screamed.

THREE

WHOOM!

A huge wall of white thundered down at us. It swallowed everything in its path. I watched it plow over my dad's old skis, toss them high in the air, and roar closer and closer.

"Noodle!" yelled Zeek. "We're doomed!"

Zeek was waiting for my brilliant plan to save us. *I* was waiting for my brilliant plan to save us.

Wump-wump-wump! The avalanche charged at us. Zeek was waiting. I was waiting.

"You're right," I cried. "We're doomed!"

Suddenly—*Thwank! Thwank!*

Two warped brown boards plunked down in the snow just inches away.

"Your skis!" cried Zeek.

My brain worked lightning fast. "Surf's up!" I yelled. In a flash we each jumped on a ski. Good thing my dad's old skis were so wide!

WHO-OOM! The wall of snow broke and crashed behind us, scooped us up, and sent us surfing down the mountainside.

Snow was still sticking to the skis, but the avalanche was pushing us so hard, even those ancient boards took off!

"Goin' for the gold!" Zeek yelled out.

We curled over and under the waves of snow like Olympic snow surfers!

"New category!" I shouted. It was incredible. We were really moving.

I figured at the rate we were going we'd be down the mountain in no time. I figured we'd end up right at the lodge, leap off the

20

skis, and dig into some birthday cake. I figured—

I figured wrong.

Just ahead was something familiar. A long shadow in the snow. The avalanche was pushing us straight for it. What *was* that thing . . . ?

"The Pit of Death!" Zeek cried.

My life flashed before my eyes—again. In three seconds I got from the hospital where I was born to the Pit of Death, where I would probably die.

Ka-Voom! The snow picked us up, and we went flying over the Pit.

My dad's skis kept going, hit the far side of the chasm, and soared high up in the air.

Zeek and I dropped straight down.

"Ahhhhhh!" we screamed as we plummeted deep into the Pit of Death!

We would have screamed the whole way down, except about halfway there—

SPLAT! SPLAT!— we crashed on a ledge.

"Ohhh!" I groaned. "Smushed again!"

I lay there in a heap for a while.

When my mashed-up brain could think again, I sat up and turned to Zeek. "Are you alive?"

"No." He sat up, dusted the snow off, and wiggled his legs. "Well, maybe I'm alive, but I'm definitely shorter than I used to be."

I looked around. The ledge led into an icy cave a few feet deep. On the back wall was an opening in the rocks about the size of a small pizza.

The cave floor was covered with a thin coating of snow that had drifted in from the chasm. Beneath that snow was total ice. I know. I slipped about a hundred times getting to my feet.

Then I saw it. Something on the wall just above the pizza hole. I slid closer to see.

It was a drawing. An old drawing. Right on the cave wall.

"Zeek, look at this. It's . . . a cave drawing! Do you know what this is?"

"A drawing some person did in a cave?"

"No, a drawing some *cave person* did in a cave! I've seen pictures like this in art books. Holy cow, there are . . . ten figures here! Boy, they're big! Cavemen, I bet. And these things are their clubs. Big clubs. Big hair, too. Very hairy."

"All right, let me see." Zeek slid over. He studied the drawing. "What's with this big guy's feet? They're really long." He pointed to two things coming out from one of the caveman's legs.

I thought for a second. "He's got skis on!"

"The ones your dad gave you?"

I made a face. "If only we could get back to the lodge and tell everybody—"

"The lodge!" cried Zeek. "I'm missing my party!" He slumped on the floor. "At this very moment, Emily is probably eating all my cake. She loves cake like you love waffles."

I felt sorry for Zeek. Then I had a brilliant idea. I stooped down and started pushing some snow into a pile on the floor.

"What are you doing?"

"Making a snow cake. For the birthday boy!" Zeek laughed. We both slid around the floor and pushed more snow into a pile.

Suddenly, we stopped. We looked at the icy floor. We looked *into* the icy floor.

"Zeek?" I whispered. "I think there's something under the ice here."

We stood up to look at the dark shape.

Zeek shuddered and backed away. "It's a bear," he whispered. "A huge bear!"

"Zeek . . ." I said.

"Noodle, don't even say it. It's a bear, okay?"

I just pointed down at the ice. "Bears have fur, Zeek. That's not fur. It's—"

"Don't say it!"

"Zeek, it's a . . . a . . . beard!"

FOUR

Zeek backed up and hit the wall behind him. "Oh, man! Of all the caves in this mountain, we had to fall into the one with the frozen dead guy!"

I brushed away the snow to get a better look at the shape. It was a guy, all right. But not just any guy. Big jaw. Big teeth. Big club. Big hair.

"Zeek!" I cried. "This is a cave guy! In fact, I bet this is one of the cave guys in that drawing. The really big one with the club. This is incredible! A real live cave guy—except that he's dead, of course."

"Maybe he's not dead," Zeek said, leaning over the shape.

I stopped brushing the ice. "No way."

"It could happen," Zeek said. "I saw this movie once—"

Uh-oh. Red alert. When Zeek goes into a panic, he always talks about some totally impossible movie thing as if it could really happen.

Also, his voice gets funny—kind of high and squeaky.

"It was about a huge fly trapped in the ice—"

"Zeek," I said, "this caveman's been frozen for probably fifty thousand years."

"So was this fly! And then some crazy scientist unfreezes it and trains it to attack and—"

Zeek was getting totally carried away. I had to go into my teacher voice, quick. I do that when Zeek gets a nutty idea into his head and it takes over. Sometimes, it's the only thing that works.

"Now, now, Zeek," I said, talking like our teacher, Mr. Strunk. "The caveman is not really alive, you know? I'm sure there's a perfectly normal explanation—"

"Normal?" he squeaked. "You think any of this is *normal*?"

Red alert, level two. The squeaky voice.

"Zeek Pilinsky, take your seat."

"Look, Noodle, the ski lift breaks, I lose my skis, an avalanche nearly kills us, you lose your skis, we get pushed off a cliff, we fall almost to the center of the earth, but—oh, great!—we get mushed flat on a ledge instead, and then we discover a fifty-million-year-old dead guy who at any moment could get up and—"

"Fifty thousand," I said.

"What?" he squeaked.

"Fifty-thousand-year-old dead guy, not fifty-million-year-old dead guy."

"It's the DEAD GUY part I don't like!—"

RRRR. The cave started to rumble around us.

"What was that?" Zeek's eyes got wide.

The rumbling got closer.

"Noodle, I don't like this. The ice on that guy is not all that thick. Any second it could just—"

KKRRRREEEEEEEKKKKKK!

A narrow crack split the ice right over the caveman's face.

"HE'S ALIVE!" Zeek screamed. "JUST LIKE THAT FROZEN FLY!"

The ice crackled across the cave floor.

The walls shook. Icicles and rocks crashed down from above.

"Cave-in!" I shouted. "Let's get out of here!"

"Great plan," Zeek cried. "Where?"

He had a point. On one side of us was the Pit of Death. On the other was the pizza-sized hole in the wall.

I did some quick thinking. Pit of Death? Pizza? Pit of Death? Pizza?

I went for the pizza. "This way!" I shouted.

We dodged the falling rocks and clambered up the wall. We both jumped for the pizza hole.

Suddenly—*KREKKK!*—the ice broke apart, and the caveman started to move!

FIVE

"**A**aaaeeeee!" screamed Zeek, as he dived into the opening.

"Eeeeeaaaaa!" I cried, as I jammed myself in next to him.

"Ugh!" we both yelled, as we stopped halfway through.

"Noodle, I'm stuck! Help!"

"I can't ! I'm stuck, too!"

We squirmed, we twisted, we tugged, we pulled. Nothing. We couldn't budge.

Our heads were sticking into total darkness. Our legs were still dangling in the caveman's cave. And something was going on back there.

"Noodle," cried Zeek, "your hipbone is

grinding into my stomach. Move it or I'll throw up!"

"Shhh! I want to hear what's going on."

Zeek swallowed loudly. I listened. The rumbling was over. No more big crashing rocks. Now it sounded like ice breaking up.

"It's him!" Zeek gasped. "He's testing out that huge club of his! Noodle, he's going to see our legs and he's going to grab them and pull us—!"

Mmm . . . mmm. Mmm-de-mmm.

Zeek got quiet. "Is that . . . humming?"

I listened closely. "Yeah. Humming. But . . ."

"A caveman who *hums*?" Zeek hissed. "Noodle, please get us out of here. Now!"

"How can I think with you spitting in my ear?" I whispered.

The ice kept cracking. The humming went on.

"I've got it!" I gasped.

"You've got a plan to get us out?"

"No, I've got that song! It's from an old TV show. I think it was called . . . *The Uggo Show*!"

Then I sang it softly.

"Back in the Age of Ice,
When weather wasn't nice,
Meet Uggo and his pals,
They're cool Neanderthals!"

I laughed. "Remember that song? It's so old!"

There was a moment of total quiet. I was sure Zeek was making one of his faces. "No kidding it's old, Noodle. *A caveman is humming it!*"

I knew a frozen dead Neanderthal caveman could *not* be humming a TV theme song. I knew that. Of course I did. I did!

"It's impossible, Zeek," I whispered. "I'm pretty sure the caveman's dead."

"Yeah, but he's humming!"

"But he's dead."

"But he's humming."

"But he's dead."

"*I don't like that combination!*" Zeek cried. He tried to move. "Another thing I don't like is your hipbone in my stomach. It's starting to give me a pain."

"Okay," I said, "just don't make any loud—"

KA-FOOM!

An explosion rocked the cave, and we blasted from the hole like human cannonballs. Tons of rocks and ice blasted from the hole, too. In fact, the hole itself got blasted away along with us!

We whizzed through the darkness.

Umph! I hit a wall and got dumped on the ground.

Umph! Zeek got dumped next to me.

I felt around in the dark. There was something hard and cold running beneath me. Something metal.

"Where are we now?" I mumbled.

Suddenly—*Flink!*—there was light next

to me. It was coming from Zeek's forehead.

"Your head!" I yelped. "It's glowing!"

"A miner's hat, Noodle! I found it over here on the ground. Here's one for you."

He passed me a hard hat with a light on the front. "Cool," I said, switching it on. "Now let's see what I'm sitting on. Shine your head over here."

Two shiny silver rails glinted in the light from our hats. The rails led back up to the blown-up cave on one side, and down past us and around a turn on the other.

"Zeek, we must be in a tunnel in the old mine I read about at the lodge. I bet these rails lead to—"

Clack-clack-clack. Grrrrr. Errch. Clack. Clack.

"What was that?" Zeek hissed, grabbing me.

I shined my light back up the tunnel to the blasted cave. There, a big, rusty tub on wheels was creaking down the rails toward us.

"A mining car," I said. "The kind they used to use to move stuff around in the old mine. The explosion must have knocked it loose."

It was a mining car, all right. And it was rolling toward us. But there was something else, too.

Something we could see in our headlights as the car got closer.

"Um . . . there's someone in it, Noodle," said Zeek quietly.

In the flickering light from our hats we could see an enormous icy shape sticking up from the mining car. Big hair. Big club. Big teeth. Big jaws.

"It's *him*!" Zeek gasped. "And he's driving!"

RRRRR! The car hit a bump on the rails and took off. It picked up speed. Lots of speed!

SHOOM! In seconds, Zeek and I were racing down the dark bumpy tunnel, trying to keep ahead of the mining car.

CLACK-CLACK-CLACK!

We stumbled into turns, over bumps, and down steep drops. The lights on our heads made crazy shadows on the rough walls as we ran. The tunnels zigzagged through the mountain like the Sling Shot ride at the Mayville carnival.

And still the mining car came at us.

I shot a look back at Uggo in the car.

He was about to mow us down.

CLACK-CLACK-UMPH!

Suddenly, I was thrown into the air.

Bong! My head hit something hard.

I heard a groan, and Zeek's headlight went out.

The last thing I saw was Uggo's huge shape lunging toward me.

Then everything went dark for me, too.

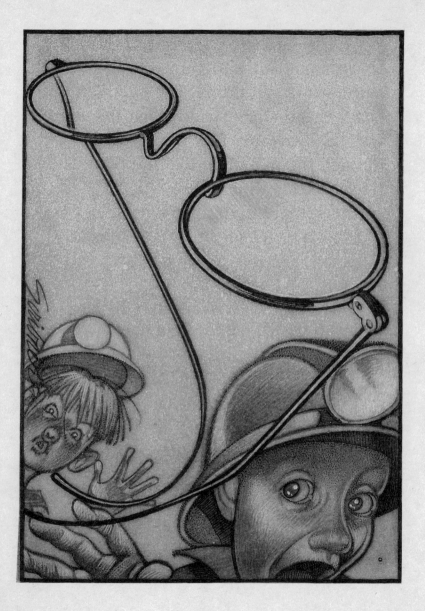

SIX

Waffles.

My brain was thinking of waffles. Maybe because when I hit whatever I hit, it made little waffle dents in my head.

Too bad my mining hat flew off just before I hit the wall. I could still hear that *Bong!* going on in my head.

I sat up and groped around in the dark. Cold rocks. Cold rails. Ice. Ice. Ice.

"Zeek?" I said.

"Uggo?" he groaned. "Is that you?"

Yeah, Zeek, the funnyman.

Flink! A light went on about twenty feet away. It was Zeek's headlamp. Then it began to flicker.

"Your light's going out," I said. "I'll try to find mine."

In the dim glow I could see that we were in a big icy cavern. The mining car—and Uggo—were nowhere in sight.

The car must have pushed Zeek out of the way and thrown me in the air. The rails ended behind me at the wall I was smushed against.

Zeek got up, wiggled, checked his arms and legs, and started along the tracks over to me.

Just as I found my mining hat on the ground, something happened.

I heard some rocks sliding and scraping.

"Noodle! I'm slipping—"

Instantly, Zeek's light did a weird zig-zag in the air and then flashed down in front of me.

"Noodle-oodle-oodle!" his cry echoed.

I grabbed for him, but I was too late. I watched his light disappear into the darkness far below.

"Zeekie!" My call bounced around and around the dark cavern.

I shined my light into the shadows. The rails that led across to the tunnel were dangling over a deep, dark chasm. Another deadly Pit!

My brain went nuts! I must have been thrown right over the chasm. But Zeek hadn't seen it!

He'd fallen between the rails straight into the pit below us. And now he was gone. On his birthday! He was lost somewhere down there. I knew for sure—

"Um . . . could I have some help here?"

Zeek?

I shined my light down. About halfway across the ravine, clutching the skinny rails, were two hands.

"Zeekie!"

KKRRR! The rails started to wobble. They were coming loose on our side of the ravine.

"The tracks are going to fall!" he screamed.

There was no time for anything fancy.

I dropped to the ground and slid out onto the tracks. Rocks and ice tumbled into the ravine. The rails sagged with the weight of both of us.

Good thing we hadn't eaten any cake yet.

I was flat on the rails, reaching out to Zeek, just like you reach for someone who's fallen through the ice at a pond.

He let go of one rail, swung up a hand and grabbed mine. He did the same with the other.

Inch by inch, I pulled him back to the ledge. We scrambled up just in time.

CRASH! The rails tore loose from the ledge, and the tangled mess of iron plunged into the darkness of the ravine. It made a horrible sound.

I was shaking all over. I was so nervous, I had to sit down.

Zeek sat next to me. "Thanks, pal. You were great."

"Two Pits of Death in one day," I said. "What are the odds?"

Zeek smiled in the light from my head. "Pretty good, if you're a Danger Guy." He gave me a slow thumbs-up sign.

I did the same. I was still shaking, though. "Zeek, I've been thinking about the cave back there. The explosion. I mean, Uggo's just a dead Neanderthal."

"You hope."

"No, listen, Zeek. Cavemen don't hum TV theme songs. You have to be alive to do that. There was someone else in that cave when we got stuck. Someone who set off that explosion. Someone who got that mining car moving. Someone in this mountain."

I tried to stand and look around, but I slipped on a patch of ice and knocked my head on the wall.

Bong! It hurt. Again.

Zeek grabbed my arm. "Hey, do that again."

I rubbed my dented head and gave him a look. "I don't think so," I said.

"No, listen. Your head bonged the wall."

"Twice."

"But, Noodle. We don't go bong when we hit *rock*, do we?" He tapped the wall. *Bong-bong!*

"It's metal!" I whispered. "A door! A secret door! I knew it! Zeek, this proves there is someone else here."

"Someone who likes caves and knows TV songs?"

"Right." I searched the wall all around the door. Then I stopped. I found what I was looking for.

I turned to Zeek and pointed to a little red button on the wall. "There's only one way to find out for sure."

Zeek looked at the red button. "What are we going to find in there, Noodle?"

I shrugged. "Could be something very

normal. Another dark tunnel, maybe. Just rocks and ice."

"Yeah, or . . . ?"

"Or, it could be something totally dangerous."

Zeek was quiet for a little while. He shook his head. Then he started to smile. "It's that danger thing, isn't it? It just takes over."

I nodded. "Yep."

Zeek zipped his jacket all the way up. I tied my crusty bootlaces tight.

We did our thumbs-up. We were ready.

I pressed the button.

VRRRRRUMP! The wall slid up and away.

Yeah, it could have been something very normal.

But it wasn't .

SEVEN

We found ourselves staring into an enormous room built right in the center of the mountain.

The craggy walls rose to a ceiling about fifty feet high. There was a skylight at the top. I could see snowflakes swirling outside. Zeek looked up at it, too. Then we stepped in slowly.

The tracks continued a few feet along the floor from the outside tunnel, then stopped. The mining car was standing just inside the door, empty.

The room beyond it was cluttered with weird scientific machinery. Big metal computers with lights and dials blinked against the far walls.

"Someone's been busy," Zeek said. "This is some kind of super laboratory."

In the middle of the room was a blackboard covered with strange mathematical symbols.

"I have a bad feeling about this," I said.

Suddenly—*VRRRMP!* A door flew open on the other side of the lab. Zeek and I dove behind a blinking machine.

The air roared with the growling and sputtering of a loud motor. I craned my neck to look.

A shiny blue snowmobile drove slowly in.

"Uh-oh," I gasped. Strapped onto the back of the snowmobile was a giant chunk of ice.

"Hey," Zeek whispered, tapping my shoulder. "I know that chunk of ice!"

We both knew that chunk of ice. It was Uggo. Still big. Still hairy. Still frozen. Just like he was fifty thousand years ago. Only now he was being driven around on a snowmobile.

And guess who was at the wheel? The clown with the pink glasses and wild hair! He wore a white lab coat and had a creepy smile on his face. His mustache was flopping up and down. He looked like someone from a bad horror movie.

Mmmm-de-mmmm. He was humming the Uggo theme song.

Zeek jabbed me in the arm. "You were right. I guess dead cave guys don't hum."

The man stopped the snowmobile, loosened the straps around Uggo, and went over to a large control panel on the wall. He pressed a button.

DJNNN! A big claw thing came down from the ceiling and closed around Uggo. It swung him over to a platform against the wall.

Zeek turned and gave me a look. "I don't like this, Nood."

He was right. It didn't look good. I tried

to check out the clown guy. Hanging from his belt was a silver pistol with blue streaks on it.

It said *Freez-Beamer* on the side.

What came next was worse. The guy looked closely at Uggo. Then he started to chuckle and giggle. Finally, he laughed out loud, shaking and twitching all over. He shook so hard, his glasses hit the floor. He twitched again, and his puffy black mustache fell off his face.

"Noodle!" Zeek gasped, "he's falling apart!"

The man shook a third time and one bushy eyebrow dangled down.

Finally—"Aaa-aaa-CHOOO!"—a supersonic sneeze echoed through the laboratory, and his big round nose came hurtling through the air.

Splat! It landed on my right ski boot.

I knew that sneeze anywhere!

"It's Mr. Vazny!" I shouted, jumping up.

"Wha—?" the man cried out. Instantly

he pulled the silver gun from his belt and swung it toward us.

But, of course, I couldn't stop blabbing.

"You're Mr. Vazny!" I shouted again. "Our old science teacher who became Dr. Morbius and tried to blow up Mayville, and Zeek and I flew all over the galaxy trying to stop you, and you almost killed us but the army came for you and locked you up, but you must have esca—"

While I was babbling, the guy's face got all weird. He went from shock to anger to kind of a nutzoid smile. His eyes became little slits. His real nose began to twitch.

Zeek nudged me. "You can stop now, Noodle. I think he remembers us."

"YOU!" the man shouted. "YOU— YOU—YOU—TROUBLEMAKERS!"

Yeah, he remembered us, all right.

He waved his silver gun in front of our faces. "So! You two Action Boys or whatever you call yourselves have gotten in my way again, haven't you?"

"Well, yes, Mr. Vazny," I said.

"It's sort of what we do," added Zeek.

The man's eyes flashed and got little again. "Did someone call me *Mr. Vazny?*"

"Yes, sir, I did," I said.

"Incorrect!" he screamed. "Would anyone else care to answer?"

"I know! I know!" Zeek raised his hand. "Is it—Dr. Morbius?"

"Wrong again!" he shrieked. He stepped over to the blackboard and spoke his name as he spelled it out. "Call me— D-o-c-t-o-r C-h-i-l-l!"

Zeek was beginning to frown like he does when Mrs. Hipple spoons out lunch on his tray and he's not sure if it's food or not.

I spoke softly. "You broke the ski lift, didn't you, Mr. Vazny—I mean, Dr. Morbius—I mean—"

"The name is Chill—Chill!—*CHILL!*"

Then he nodded slowly. "The ski lift? Yes, I needed a little part—something for my work."

Zeek raised his hand again. "But the hair?"

"Oh, this?" Chill reached up and pulled off the red wig. He tossed it to the floor. "A simple disguise to fool simple people. It helped me escape from the army jail to this old mine. I've made many improvements, as you can see!"

He waved his arms around the lab. Like on a TV game show when they show off the prizes.

"And now, it is a perfect place from which to launch my ultimate attack!"

I shot a look at Zeek. I swallowed hard. *"Attack?"* I said.

Dr. Chill turned to a huge map tacked up on the wall. He pointed to a dot on the coast.

I gasped. "But that's—Mayville!"

"So glad you've been studying your geography!"

Zeek stepped forward. "What's your horrible plan this time, Dr. Chill?"

Chill flashed a creepy grin. "I'm going to DESTROY your little town, once and for all!"

Then he laughed a terrible laugh that echoed through the laboratory. It probably echoed through all the caves in the entire mountain.

"Oh, yeah?" Zeek snarled, stepping forward. "You and what army?"

"Good one!" I said.

Chill's eyes got big and fiery. He stepped to the control panel and pressed another button.

NNNNT! Instantly, a wall opened up on the other side of the lab. A blast of cold air filled the room.

Fog poured in. The kind of icy fog that swirls around in bad horror movies.

Dr. Chill stepped back.

"Me and *this* army!" he said.

EIGHT

An icy shiver ran down my spine.

There, in the swirling fog behind Uggo, stood nine other giant frozen cavemen!

"Behold!" cried Chill. "My mighty Neanderthal army! I chopped them, cut them, and blasted them out of every frozen cave in this mountain. I brought them here—to live once more!"

He started to laugh again.

Zeek nudged me. "He thinks this is good?"

I realized that those huge hairy icy cavemen were the same ones in the cave drawing we saw.

Boy, were they big! Big hair, big jaws,

big teeth. Big clubs, too. They looked even meaner than in the drawing. It was bad news, all right. But I tried to act tough.

"Those guys are fifty thousand years old!" I said. "They can't do anything. They're ice cubes!"

"Ha-ha!" laughed Chill. "Not for long!"

NNNT! He pressed another button, and the floor in the center of the room began to slide open. Up came the most humongous, nasty-looking gun thing I ever saw.

It was huge! The long barrel had pulsating bright-orange and yellow coils running around it. Written in big red letters on the side of the gun were the words *Amazing Melt-O-Ray.*

Dr. Chill tapped the gun and began to smirk. "Three blasts from my Amazing Melt-O-Ray, and—cavemen walk the earth again!"

That's when Zeek jabbed me. His lip curled up and he squinted. He nodded down at my feet.

I looked. Chill's fake nose was still stuck to my boot. It made me feel kind of sick to see it there.

I shook my boot. The nose didn't move. I swung my boot a little more. It still stuck. Finally, I kicked way up, and the nose went soaring.

It must have spooked Dr. Chill, because when he saw this pink blobby thing flying at him, he instantly reached for the silver Freez-Beamer hanging from his belt, aimed the shiny pistol—and fired.

Zwap-o! An icy blue beam zapped through the air and caught the nose in midflight.

Plink! It dropped to the floor and shattered like glass into a thousand pink crystals.

It was totally frozen.

"No more silly moves!" Chill cried. "You see my terrible power!"

Zeek snarled. "Big deal! Like you're going to microwave these old dudes, and they're just going to wake up and start cracking dinosaur jokes."

Chill's face twisted all up. "My cavemen don't make jokes, like you funny boys!" he cried. "They know only one thing— how to destroy! These cavemen are conquerors! Killers! Ah, just imagine it— giant cavemen with giant clubs. At the Mayville Mall! At Mayville Library! At Mayville School!"

Dr. Chill laughed one of those crazy laughs he's so good at. Then he snapped a switch and the gigantic Melt-O-Ray began to sputter.

I looked over at Zeek. I could see him getting mad. He shook his head slowly and whispered, "We can't let him do this, Noodle."

Zeek was right. Mayville destroyed by a bunch of cavemen with big clubs? No way!

Chill was staring up at the Melt-O-Ray. The barrel turned bright red. He started to laugh a horrible, blood-tingling laugh.

Zeek gave me a nod. It meant he was ready.

I was ready, too.

I smiled inside. We were a team. There wasn't anybody like us. I gave Zeek a little thumbs-up.

Zeek nodded.

"Let's bust him, Noodle!"

"Now!" I shouted.

We jumped into action. Zeek dived for the Melt-O-Ray, and I lunged at Dr. Chilibean.

It was a perfect plan. Except for one thing.

The second I leaped up, I tumbled like a rock.

"Umph!" I groaned. "My boots! They're untied again!"

Zeek was halfway across the room already, leaping over lab equipment.

But Chill was too fast for either of us. The instant we moved, he turned his Freez-Beamer pistol at us and pulled the trigger.

ZWAP-O!

There was a flash.

There was a scream.

Zeek stopped leaping over lab equipment.

He shivered. He got all stiff and crusty. He didn't move. Zeek was frozen!

NINE

"**Z**eeeeeeeekie!" I screamed.

But Zeek didn't answer. He didn't budge. He didn't even breathe. Squiggly blue lines of electricity sizzled all over him.

He was covered with ice crystals. His Danger Guy jacket, his mask, his ski pants.

Everything was frosty and white.

I stumbled over to him. Dr. Chill just kept giggling to himself. "Your friend is very . . . how do you children say it—*cool!*" He laughed.

I couldn't believe it. Zeek was frozen stiff.

There was a dark blast hole right

through his Danger Guy jacket. Chill's Freez-Beamer had shot straight at his heart.

"Zeek?" I whispered right to his face. "Can you hear me?"

Nothing. No answer. He didn't move at all.

Me and my stupid old boots!

A big lump swelled in my throat. My friend was frozen, my best friend in the whole world.

I brushed some ice crystals off his jacket.

Zeek stared past me. His eyes were glassy. His fingers were cold, stiff, and spread out, like one of those mime guys trapped in an invisible box.

I started to get really mad.

Dr. Chill must have known what I was thinking, because he flipped a switch and that claw thing swung over and grabbed me. *Zzzzt!* It picked me up in the air—and stopped. I dangled.

Chill laughed, sneezed, and went back to the huge Melt-O-Ray's controls. He aimed the barrel at Uggo and the other cavemen.

This is impossible, I thought. It'll never work.

Slowly Chill pushed a giant lever forward and the red coils started to glow. "Live again, my giant Neanderthals!"

KA-ZAP!

A powerful red blast flashed at the cavemen. They sizzled all over. They began to drip.

But what if it did work? I looked over at Zeek, all frosty and still. Maybe Chill *could* do it. I could see it all now. "Monster Cavemen Destroy Peaceful City!"

I imagined Uggo and his pals marching down Main Street with their giant clubs. I shuddered.

KA-ZAAAP! The second blast hit the Neanderthals. Small pools of water spread out on the floor. The cavemen were starting to slide a little on the icy floor.

"Yes!" Chill laughed. "Even now they begin to live! One more blast, and it's Bye-bye, Mayville!"

It was only a matter of seconds now. The Melt-O-Ray was rumbling. In fact, the whole laboratory was rumbling. The computers were sizzling and sputtering. The lab was heating up.

"This whole place is going to blow!" I cried. Then it hit me. The avalanche that nearly killed us had been caused by Dr. Chill and his stupid ray gun! One more avalanche like that and—the lodge would be destroyed! Zeek's family!

No way! Chill had already frozen my best friend. I couldn't let him get Zeek's family, too!

It came to me in an instant. *Dr. Chill must be stopped*. I didn't know how I would ever pull it off, but I had to try. I was the only one left.

I had to do it. For Zeek.

The Melt-O-Ray got louder and hotter. The final blast was coming. It had to be now.

I scanned Zeek's face. Even though I knew he couldn't see me, I gave him a thumbs-up.

That's when I noticed something strange about Zeek. Something about his face. It was different.

It was one of those funny little smile things at the corners of his mouth. The kind he does from across the room in Mr. Strunk's class. The kind that always makes me laugh.

But—how? I thought. He's frozen solid!

Then, so slowly that only I could see it, Zeek lifted his thumb up.

He was alive!

I didn't know how—but it didn't matter.

Zeek was alive! Ya-hoo! The boys were back!

Meanwhile, Chill laughed louder and louder as the Melt-O-Ray turned white-hot.

The heat was incredible.

If it didn't cool down soon, it would—

Cool down? Wait a second.

I looked up. All the way up. To the ceiling. To the skylight. To the icy snow swirling outside.

Yes! In a fraction of a second I had it all worked out. An incredible total action plan! Well, almost total. I still had to figure out a couple of tiny details.

I nodded a small nod at Zeek and motioned with my eyes over to the Melt-O-Ray, then up to the skylight, then to Uggo, then to the main control panel on the wall.

Zeek knew exactly what I meant. He was reading my mind. Yeah, we were a team all right! The best team in the world.

ZZZZZ! The Melt-O-Ray was glowing white-hot. Dr. Chill was going for the firing lever.

I remembered what Zeek had said

about saving the surprises for the bad guys. Well, this was one bad dude. And we had one big surprise for him!

I nodded at Zeek. He was ready.

So was I.

"Party time!" I cried out.

TEN

Our timing was incredible. Zeek and I blasted into action as if we were one person.

Dr. Chill wasn't expecting us, especially Zeek, to move at all. So when we exploded into motion, old Chillface was totally surprised.

"B—b—back to your seats!" he screamed.

Ha! As Zeek dashed for the main control panel, I breathed out, got skinny, and—*slurp!*—I slipped through the fingers of the ugly claw and hit the floor running.

Well, sliding, actually. The floor was pretty slippery. I skidded, did a weird leap like an out-of-control figure skater, and landed with both feet on the back of the Amazing Melt-O-Ray!

FWWAAPP-O! The third and most powerful blast shot out, just as the white-hot barrel swung up to the ceiling—

CRASH! The ray hit the skylight. Glass tinkled to the floor.

Suddenly—*WHOOOMP!*—about a ton of heavy white snow dumped into the lab. The red-hot Melt-O-Ray hissed and sputtered and froze up! Icicles formed all over it. The rumbling stopped.

"Yahoo!" I shouted. "My plan actually worked!"

Huge drifts of snow buried the cavemen and—*Errch!*—stopped them cold.

"No!" screamed Dr. Chill. "Awake, my mighty cavemen!"

"Sorry, Doc," cried Zeek, diving in midair for the control panel. "They're taking a nap! They're on ice! Forever!"

Yeah, that was Zeek, some kind of

superhero! Except that on his way down he caught Uggo in the shoulder, just as the snow was covering the other cavemen. *Umph!*

Uggo slid forward in a pool of water and started to glide across the lab.

Zeek slammed against the control panel buttons and—*zip-zip-zip!*—a huge door on the far side of the lab slid open.

Chill went nuts! He whipped out his Freez-Beamer pistol and started firing at Zeek and me.

"Take that! And that!" he cried, as he blasted at us again and again. But we were moving too fast to get iced.

Finally, Zeek took a running leap, dropped to his knees, and slid across to me.

"Glad to have you back!" I said, with a smile.

"Glad to be back," said Zeek. "What's our escape plan?"

KA-ZAP! A blast zinged near our heads.

My smile faded as I ducked. "Bad news. I never really got to the escape part."

"Oh," said Zeek.

Suddenly— *Thwank! Thwank!* Two brown chewed-up boards dropped from the skylight and bounced across the floor.

I looked at Zeek. He looked at me.

"My skis!" I shouted.

"I think they're trying to tell us something!"

"Like, here's our ride?"

We jumped on the skis to make our escape.

They didn't budge.

"We're doomed!" cried Zeek.

ZAAAP! Chill's freeze shot missed us but hit a pool of water. The whole floor froze instantly into a sheet of ice.

Zeek smiled. "Should we thank him now?"

"Later!" I cried. We pushed on the skis.

Umph! Something knocked us down.

I looked up, expecting to see Dr. Chill standing over us with his ugly silver ray gun. I expected him to sneeze a couple of times, then zap us stiff.

I expected wrong.

It was Uggo! His big frozen shape slid slowly by us and right onto my dad's skis! They stuck to his icy feet. Then he started gliding toward the door on the far side of the lab.

"Grab him!" I shouted to Zeek.

Zeek's eyes bugged. "Uggo? No way!"

Zzzwap! Chill blasted the air near Zeek's head.

Zeek didn't think twice. He pushed me onto the skis behind Uggo. Then he jumped on behind me. We slid through the door and down a dark tunnel. We picked up speed. Then we *really* picked up speed. We were flying.

Rrrrrr! We heard a growl behind us. It was Dr. Chill on his snowmobile.

"Hurry, Noodle!" shouted Zeek.

"Hurry, Uggo!" I shouted, as a blue blast whizzed past my ear.

Dr. Chill's snowmobile closed in. He was gaining on us with every second.

The tunnel was ending. There was nothing but darkness ahead. I closed my eyes as Chill pulled the trigger.

ELEVEN

ZAAAAAAP!

There was a bright light.

I felt cold all over.

For the third time that day, my whole life flashed before me.

Three strikes, you're out. I'm dead!

"Noodle!" yelled Zeek. "Open your eyes!"

"Wha—?" I opened my eyes.

Sunlight and snow!

Cold mountain air!

We were outside!

I shot a look behind me. Zeekie was right there. "Hot dog!" I shouted. "We're not dead!"

We zoomed down the mountain—two kids and a frozen caveman on one set of skis! We were incredible!

But—*thwaaaaap-o!*—Chill was still hot on our heels, firing away, and gaining.

Suddenly, there was a big bump ahead of us.

And I mean a BIG BUMP!

"Uggo, turn!"

But Uggo didn't turn. He was dead, after all. We headed right for the bump.

FLOOO-OOMP! We hit the bump, and Zeek and I went flying off the skis.

Uggo kept going.

It was amazing to see a frozen dead guy on skis. He raced down the mountain like an Olympic champion. Snow was spraying out behind each ski. He shot down the slopes faster and faster. My dad would have been proud.

"He's going for the gold," I said.

"Yeah," said Zeek, "amazing at his age."

"Plus, he's dead," I said.

 84

Then Uggo flew high over a ridge and disappeared down the other side.

Crunch! We heard ice shattering. Then the skis popped up and landed—*Flunk! Flunk!*—in the snow at the top of the ridge.

Suddenly, we heard a roar off to the side. It was Dr. Chill! He was coming in for the kill!

Zeek instantly bent down and gathered up a handful of snow. "Stand back, Noodle. This is what I'm famous for, remember?"

How could I forget? The Pilinsky fast-ball. Zeek packed the snow until it turned to ice.

"Let him have it, Zeekie!" I cried.

Zeek powered up, pulled back, and fired.

The snowball shot across the mountain. *FWAMP!*

Direct hit! Right into Chill's controls. The snowmobile lurched into a deep snowdrift and stopped. Dr. Chill was buried up to his nose.

He yelled out something, then fell back into the snow.

I turned to Zeek. "Did he say something about a surprise quiz?"

Zeek smiled and shrugged. "I think we just had it, Noodle, and the teacher failed!"

I looked down the mountain and saw my dad's skis sticking up over the ridge. "Let's check out Uggo!"

When we got to where our favorite caveman had crashed, Zeek and I stared into the snow.

Our mouths dropped wide open.

We just stared and stared. We didn't breathe.

We were still like that when the rescue team came for us and Dr. Chill. We didn't even say hello. We couldn't. Our mouths were still hanging open.

They didn't close until an hour later,

around some delicious double-chocolate birthday cake.

Zeek and I wolfed down most of it while everyone stared.

After a while, we began to talk. We told them about everything—especially our discovery at the very end.

"Footprints," said Zeek quietly.

"Giant footprints," I said. "In the snow. Heading away from the empty hole."

Zeek's mom and dad just stared at us, as if they were in shock.

Emily made a strange face. "You mean, Uggo is walking around out there?"

I nodded. " 'Ancient Caveman Lives!' "

It was incredible to think about.

No one said anything for a long time.

Finally I turned to Zeek. "But one thing I don't get. Why didn't you really get frozen when Chill blasted you? I thought you were iced for sure."

Zeek smiled. "Almost," he said. "But you saved me."

"Me?" I said.

He dug into his jacket pocket and pulled out a crumpled piece of gold foil. "My Olympic medal, remember?"

He handed the medal over to me with a smile. It was the foil from my ice cream bar. There was a black mark right in the center where Dr. Chill's Freez-Beamer had blasted it.

"I did feel weird," Zeek went on. "But mostly I was faking it. It's like we said, we save the surprises for the bad guys."

I nodded slowly. "It's that danger thing, I guess. It's in our blood."

Zeek gave me one of those tiny smiles. Then he said, "You know, Noodle, it *was* pretty dangerous today. It will probably be dangerous tomorrow, too. That's the good news."

"Yeah," I said. Then I thought about it. "But what's the bad news?"

Zeek broke into a big smile. He almost didn't have to say it. I knew what he was thinking. I knew, because I was thinking the same thing.

"There isn't any bad news," he said.

The sun was just setting behind the big mountain. We were packing up to drive home.

I thought about all the amazing stuff Zeek and I had been through.

"Yeah, tomorrow," I said. "We get to do it all again. "

Don't miss the next dangerous adventure . . .

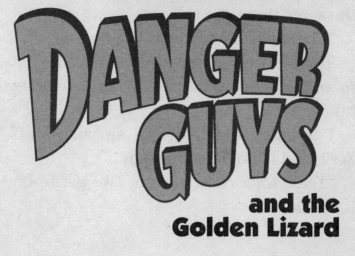

DANGER GUYS

and the Golden Lizard

"Tomorrow," Mrs. Emerson told the audience, "we go in search of the mysterious Golden Lizard, deep in the jungles of Central America."

"And what will make our expedition even more exciting," Mr. Emerson said, "is that we'll be joined by a couple of junior explorers."

I froze.

"A couple of very active young adventurers," Mrs. Emerson added.

"Z-Z-Zeek?" I said. But Zeek's mouth was hanging wide open.

"A couple of Danger Guys!"